To
2022

Pig Makes Art

written by **LAURA GEHL**   illustrated by **FRED BLUNT**

Ready-to-Read

Simon Spotlight

New York   London   Toronto   Sydney   New Delhi

Here is a list of all the words you will find in this book. Sound them out before you begin reading the story.

Names:

Cat   Pig

SIMON SPOTLIGHT
An imprint of Simon & Schuster Children's Publishing Division
1230 Avenue of the Americas, New York, New York 10020
This Simon Spotlight edition May 2022
Text copyright © 2022 by Laura Gehl
Illustrations copyright © 2022 by Fred Blunt

For information about special discounts for bulk purchases, please contact Simon & Schuster
Special Sales at 1-866-506-1949 or business@simonandschuster.com.
Manufactured in the United States of America 0322 LAK
2 4 6 8 10 9 7 5 3 1
Library of Congress Cataloging-in-Publication Data
Names: Gehl, Laura, author. | Blunt, Fred, illustrator. Title: Pig makes art / by Laura Gehl ;
illustrated by Fred Blunt. Description: Simon Spotlight edition. | New York : Simon Spotlight,
2022. | Summary: "Pig makes art. Cat does not like the art. Will Cat have a change of heart?"—
Provided by publisher. Identifiers: LCCN 2021041102 | ISBN 9781534499522 (paperback)
| ISBN 9781534499539 (hardcover) | ISBN 9781534499546 (ebook) Subjects: LCSH:
Swine—Juvenile fiction. | Cats—Juvenile fiction. | Friendship—Juvenile fiction. | Readers
(Primary) | CYAC: Pigs—Fiction. | Cats—Fiction. | Friendship—Fiction. | LCGFT: Animal
fiction. | Readers (Publications) Classification: LCC PZ7.G2588 Pi 2022 | DDC [E]—dc23
LC record available at https://lccn.loc.gov/2021041102

Word families:

"-akes" →	makes	takes	wakes	
"-og" →	dog	fog	frog	log
"-ots" →	dots	lots	spots	

Sight words:

| a | and | of | on |
| the | up | | |

Bonus words:

| adds | art | nap | runs | snorts |

Ready to go? Happy reading!

Don't miss the questions about the story
on the last page of this book.

Pig makes art.

Cat snorts.

Pig adds a dog.

Cat snorts.

Pig adds fog
and a log.

Cat snorts.

Pig adds a frog
on the log.

Cat snorts.

Cat takes a nap.

Pig adds dots.

Pig adds lots
and lots of dots.

Pig adds spots.

Pig adds lots and
lots of spots.

Pig snorts.

Cat wakes up.

Cat snorts.

Pig runs.

Cat makes art.

Pig snorts.

Pig makes art.

Cat makes art.

Now that you have read the story, can you answer these questions?

1. Which character makes art at the beginning of the story?

2. Why does Pig paint dots and spots on Cat?

3. In this story you read the words "makes" and "takes" and "wakes." Those words rhyme. Can you think of other words that rhyme with "makes" and "takes" and "wakes"?

Great job!
You are a reading star!